HUNGRY NEXT DOOR

HUNGRY NEXT DOOR

By

Tia Guay

Illustrator: Danitza Romero - Anima 3D

Hungry Next Door
Tia Guay

There once was a boy named Eric. He had black hair, brown eyes, and he always wore his favorite blue shorts and a red shirt. He lived in New York City with his mom.

1

Eric's mom did not have a job and could not provide food for Eric.

Most nights, Eric would have a slice of bread for dinner because his mom could not afford a full meal.

3

Eric was always so excited to go to school.

At school, Eric would eat breakfast and lunch from the cafeteria.

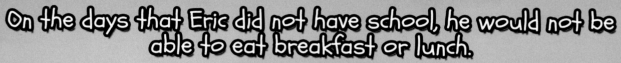

On the days that Eric did not have school, he would not be able to eat breakfast or lunch.

He would only have that one piece of bread for dinner.

Each and every day, Eric's stomach would growl...

However, today was not an ordinary day for Eric.

When Eric was taking a walk around his neighborhood,
he saw a boy walking in front of him.

As he got closer, he realized that this boy had brown hair and big blue eyes.

Eric knew that he wanted to talk to the boy, so
he built up all of his courage and said,
"Hi my name is Eric. What's your name?"

16

The brown-haired boy looked into Eric's eyes and said, "Hi Eric, my name is Jesse."

17

At first, the boys did not know what to say or what to do.

All of a sudden, Jesse heard a strange noise coming from Eric's stomach.

19

Eric explained that his mom did not have enough money
to buy food because she did not have a job.

Before Jesse had the chance to ask Eric
more questions, a voice rang out from the distance,
"Time to come inside now Jesse!" It was
Jesse's mom. Jesse had to go inside for dinner.

23

Jesse waved goodbye to Eric and ran inside his house.

Eric continued to walk back to his house as it was starting to get dark.

Once Jesse got back home, he came up with a plan.

Jesse was going to host food drives to provide food for people in need.

27

He asked his friends and family for donations.

He walked all around the neighborhood and persuaded them to donate.

After one month, he had raised 1,000 food items!

He was now able to provide food for Eric and his mom. The remainder of the food would go to anyone in the city that was in need.

Jessie drove with his mom to deliver the food to all of the houses in the neighborhood.

33

After the food was delivered, Eric woke up like any other day.

He got dressed, brushed his teeth, grabbed his backpack, and was ready to go to school.

When he walked into the kitchen, something was different...

There was a HUGE pile of food sitting on the counter!

He grabbed a plastic plate from the closet and began to scoop the food on the plate.

While eating, Eric noticed a note clipped onto one of the bags of food.

Eric was so excited because he was now able to have three full meals each day.

Eric realized that he should be grateful for all that he now had.